THE MYSTERY
OF THE
MILITARY ESTABLISHMENT

VIVAAN CHOPRA

Copyright © Vivaan Chopra 2024
All Rights Reserved.

ISBN
Hardcase 979-8-89588-944-2
Paperback 979-8-89322-602-7

This book has been published with all efforts taken to make the material error-free after the consent of the author. However, the author and the publisher do not assume and hereby disclaim any liability to any party for any loss, damage, or disruption caused by errors or omissions, whether such errors or omissions result from negligence, accident, or any other cause.

While every effort has been made to avoid any mistake or omission, this publication is being sold on the condition and understanding that neither the author nor the publishers or printers would be liable in any manner to any person by reason of any mistake or omission in this publication or for any action taken or omitted to be taken or advice rendered or accepted on the basis of this work. For any defect in printing or binding the publishers will be liable only to replace the defective copy by another copy of this work then available.

Contents

Acknowledgement

I would like to thank my family especially my parents, Manjul and Uma Chopra, for inspiring me to write my first book.

A very special thank you to my twin brother, Ishaan Chopra, who was also coincidentally writing a book at the same time as me. Both of us inspired each other, though our stories were different.

My special gratitude to the teachers of my school, Bishop Cottons Boys' School, for developing my abilities and instilling the confidence to write a book. In addition, I would also thank Roots Football Club for teaching me discipline and patience.

I also wanted to thank Ms Priyanka Reddy for the nice cover design and illustrations for my book.

Chapter 1

A Surprise for the Adventurers

"Hey, catch the ball. Don't be so slow," Johann said to Phillip, who laughed and replied, "Sure."

Johann playfully threw the ball towards his friend. The strong wind blew the ball away, as it was a soft beach ball.

"Oh, the ball is going somewhere else," Bastian complained.

"Now someone has to find the ball," Manuel grumbled.

"Anyone saw where it went?" asked Albert.

"I think it went over there on that yacht," said Jurgen.

"Who'll get it?" asked Phillip.

Nobody wanted to go, as the yacht was on the far side of the beach, and they did not feel like walking all the way over there. In the end, Manuel said, "Johann should go. After all, he threw the ball."

"Okay, fine, I'll go. You're right, I threw it," Johann readily agreed.

Johann cautiously walked to the yacht, as the sand was warm and slippery, and the yacht was at the edge of the water. Johann took care so that he did not fall into the water. He reached the specific yacht where Jurgen told him the ball had gone. Johann quietly got on the yacht. A quick glance showed that there was no activity on the yacht, and he saw the ball lying near a large crate on the far side of the deck. Johann made his way across and picked up the ball. Suddenly, a door opened, and he heard voices and footsteps. He hid behind the large crate. "Oh no, I hope they didn't see me. They shouldn't find me. They'll think I'm a burglar trying to steal," thought Johann.

Johann cautiously peeped out and saw a thin, tall man who had a cruel face with a moustache and a goatee. The man had a thin, angular face with sharp, piercing eyes and was

The **Adventurers** were playing on the beach

bald. The man was wearing a good-quality coat and had a thick pair of glasses peeping out of his coat pocket. He was wearing white gloves and shoes that looked like the ones used in a science lab for experiments. Johann thought, "This person looks like a scientist."

"Watch out, the police are very cautious," said the man on the yacht. The other man replied, "Sure. We have to be very careful." The second man spoke with a Spanish accent.

Johann thought while hiding behind the crate, "He must be from Spain or South America. Many people are talking about a large number of South Americans immigrating to European countries, which are well-developed countries with better living conditions. Especially coastal areas like the north of Germany have better jobs that pay more, thus helping South Americans escape the political situation, the dangerous way of living, and the poverty back home. They come over here and do menial jobs like helpers on small yachts. This looks like a pretty run-down yacht." Johann further thought, still hiding behind the crate, "I wonder who this man is? He looks like a scientist! And why this other man has a South

American accent? Also, what did he mean by that sentence of being careful from the police."

The two men went back into the control room. Johann was relieved and quietly got off the yacht, clutching the ball in his hand.

While getting back to the shore, Johann saw the name of the yacht – *The Southern Star*. "It must be from South America," he thought. He walked slowly, contemplating what he had seen and heard.

He reached back, and Jurgen said impatiently, "What took you so long?" Johann told his story, and Albert said, "Very suspicious."

It was the first day of the boys' summer vacation, and they had gone to the beach to enjoy and play.

They were a group of six boys who lived in Nordreich, a small town in northern Germany bordering the sea. They all lived near the beach, in houses next to each other. Their parents were business partners, and they had gone on a business trip.

There were six of them – Johann, Jurgen, Albert, Manuel, Phillip, and Bastian.

Johann Muller was a very clever boy with jet-black hair and was seventeen years old. He was very brave and equanimous. He was always cool-headed and would think things through before acting. He was the leader of the boys' group, and each one of them looked up to him for suggestions.

Jurgen Strasse was a seventeen-year-old boy. He had black hair and was very resourceful. He was known for being able to use any material around him to fix a mechanical issue. He was like the troubleshooter of the group.

Albert Heinze was an eighteen-year-old boy, who was very tall and thin. He had blond hair and was very smart. He could think his way out of any problem. He was also called Smart Kid by his friends.

Manuel Stein was also eighteen years old. He had blond hair and was very strong. Even though he was strong, he did not use his strength to hurt people; instead, he helped them. Manuel was known as the Iron Man of the group.

Bastian Hanise had just turned sixteen and was a tall boy for his age. He had brown hair and was very helpful to his friends. He was known for helping anyone he saw in need or who asked for his help.

Phillip Manste was a sixteen-year-old boy, who was the shortest in the group. He had curly brown hair and was very kind. Philip was the most liked boy of the group, being the youngest and shortest of the group. He was also very good at sketching and loved to sketch his friends.

All the six boys were very good friends, staying close by in the small town of Nordreich, located in northern Germany. They were known as intelligent and fun-loving boys. The boys were always looking out for some mystery and jokingly called themselves '*Adventurers*'.

Chapter 2

Coincidence or Not?

It was a nice sunny day with a clear sky.

"Let's go and watch a movie at the new cinema hall on the outskirts of the town, followed by a walk in the old part of the town. It's also been a long time since we went to that part of the town," Johann said excitedly. All of them jumped at the idea and left for the cinema hall to watch the latest action movie.

On their way back from the cinema hall, while enjoying the beauty of the old town, they came across a building which looked quite new. It was strange that a new building had suddenly popped up in the old part of the town. As the boys observed the building, they noticed the guards patrolling the establishment armed with weapons. It seemed like a military establishment. The boys checked around and looked up, and their guess was correct. It was a military establishment.

"On this piece of land, there used to be an old, abandoned mansion, which was said to be haunted when we last came this way, and now it seems to be a military establishment," Jurgen said in a surprised tone. Johann suddenly jumped and exclaimed, "This is the same man I saw on the yacht!" as he pointed towards a man wearing a laboratory coat and coming out of the building.

"Are you sure?" asked Jurgen.

"I'm sure it is him. I won't forget his face," said Johann.

"Well, he seems to be working in this military establishment," Jurgen said.

A disturbing thought came to Johann's mind. He said, "Those words I heard on the yacht. He may be plotting something wrong at the military establishment."

"It probably is a coincidence," Manuel said casually.

"Or you may have been imagining things," Bastian suggested.

Albert interrupted, "Let's go home; it's getting late." The boys decided to go home. Johann suggested, "On the way back home, we should go to the beach towards the same yacht."

They were surprised. At the beach, this time, they saw two men strangely hurrying towards the shore, where the yacht was anchored.

"Hey, look," Johann said, pointing at the men. "That was the same man I saw on the yacht the other day and also outside the establishment. But who is the second man?"

"Wait here and see what I do," Johann said in one breath and hurriedly rushed across and bumped into one of the men. A paper had fallen from that man's hand and Johann picked it up and gave it back while having a quick look at the paper. After that, he also stole a careful glance at both the men. He also looked at the yacht and saw another man looking intently from the yacht. This man seemed to be the same person he had seen earlier on the yacht. It looked as if he was from South America.

Johann reached back to his friends and said, "It was the same yacht, *The Southern Star.*

This is the same man I saw on the yacht!
Johann exclaimed
MILITARY ESTABLISHMENT

I have now seen three suspicious men connected to the yacht and had a good look at them."

"Can you sketch them, Phillip? You are very good at this," asked Johann. "The one I bumped into just now is a man, about five feet nine inches tall and is stout. He has a beard and wears glasses." He further added, "The man we can see on the yacht right now is short – about five feet seven inches in height. He is dark-skinned and stout and has black hair. I wonder if he is from South America. He must have been the second man on the yacht yesterday, the one whose voice I would have heard." Johann said, "The third man whom I saw on the yacht yesterday and also in the military establishment in lab clothes is a tall man of about six feet two inches. He has an angular face with a moustache and a goatee."

"How are these sketches of the three suspicious men?" Phillip asked excitedly after spending some time sketching them with inputs from Johann. Philip had this unusual habit of carrying all his sketching material, which was always handy, with him in his small shoulder bag. So, it proved very fruitful on that day.

"You got them correct. We'll go to the police station today, and we can show the descriptions of these men. This will help the police to investigate further into this matter, and hopefully, nothing wrong will happen at the military establishment," Johann replied.

"Oh, and when I bumped into the man, I heard him speaking of documents, and the paper I picked up looked something like a blueprint of a big building," Johann said.

"Could they be planning to steal some documents from the military establishment and give it to some foreign military power? Johann saw the same man at the yacht and at the new building," Jurgen wondered aloud.

"Is it a coincidence that Johann saw the same person at both places? The same person who seemed to be worried about the police? We better tell the police about this," Albert said.

They all went to the police station and met the Chief of Police, Mr Ruediger Mertens, and told him the whole story, starting with the ball going on the yacht. Ruediger Mertens was the head of the police station in the town of Nordreich, the hometown of all the boys.

Mr Mertens laughed sarcastically after hearing the whole story from the boys and said, "What would you know about the military establishment? Narrating some story and wasting my time," and then the Chief of Police suddenly left the police station saying he had some very important work.

The boys felt disheartened and shocked by the strange response from the Chief of Police, Mr Mertens.

Chapter 3

Interesting New Information

The group of six boys, who used to call themselves *Adventurers*, were feeling down and dejected the next day morning. While the boys were having breakfast, they decided that it was time for them to act on their own. They felt that the Chief of Police had not taken them seriously, and thus, he was not willing to act on their information. However, the *Adventurers* were convinced with their findings and were sure that there was something suspicious about the yacht and the men on board.

"Johann, do you think we should keep an eye on the men and the yacht?" asked Jurgen.

Johann was quiet for some time and then suddenly spoke excitedly. "Yes, we should do it. We also should enquire about the yacht," Johann said and then quickly explained the plan.

Johann started explaining his idea in detail to others in order to clarify their roles, "Okay, Bastian, you go and stay at the shore and look out for the yacht."

"Phillip, you go and stay near the police station. If you see or hear of any suspicious activity, tell us," continued Johann.

"Jurgen will follow the men. See if they take any detours. Manuel, you should enquire about the yacht. Albert, you stand outside the military establishment and see who is coming in and going out," said Johann.

"I'll go inside the establishment undercover, disguised as a guard," Johann finally concluded.

They all got ready for their duties as per the plan. All the six boys gave each other a high-five and excitedly set off to carry out their jobs.

Manuel set off and casually asked the man, who was in charge of docking the yachts, "Can you tell me about the yacht, *The Southern Star*? This looks different from others."

The man on the dock replied, "*The Southern Star*. Well, it's a strange boat. Comes in the middle of the night and leaves before noon the following day. Three men come on it. They have strange complexion, South American, I think. These men meet other well-dressed men, and they talk for some time. Then, the yacht goes away. Comes every week or so. It is registered under a person named Carlo."

Meanwhile, Bastian went to the beach and was on the lookout for the yacht.

Phillip went to the police station and sat on a bench just outside.

Albert and Jurgen went to the military establishment and stood outside to carry out their plans. Albert's role was to stand guard outside the establishment. Jurgen's plan was to follow the suspicious men if they left the establishment towards the yacht.

Johann came later to the military establishment after wearing a guard's uniform. Johann had played the part of a policeman in his school play. He was happy to use the uniform for a good purpose. Johann made some small changes in the uniform to match the actual uniform that the guard of the military establishment was wearing. He wore the uniform and was ready to act like a guard. When Johann reached the military establishment, Jurgen told him the guards followed a rotational system of coming and going after periods of one hour each.

"Okay, I just have one hour to snoop around. Now I'll go," thought Johann. Johann carefully climbed the fence to the point where it was slightly open and went inside. He saw only one guard on duty and went up to him. Johann said, "I have to take your place, you can go now." The guard left, and Johann was delighted. The first part of his plan had worked.

Johann confidently went inside the establishment, posing as a guard. Once inside, he snooped around and came to an office. Little did he know that it was the office of the head of the operation. There was a nameplate in front of the office mentioning 'Sebastian Schmidt'. Johann guessed that Sebastian Schmidt was heading the military establishment. It struck Johann that he could narrate the whole story to the head of the establishment.

Suddenly, Johann heard footsteps and saw the Chief of Police, Mr Mertens. "Where are you going?" Johann asked confidently to the Chief of Police. The Chief replied rudely, "To Mr. Sebastian Schmidt, head of this military establishment," and went into the room.

Johann pressed his ear to the door and heard a conversation between the head of the military establishment and the Chief of Police. Johann wanted to make sure he was able to hear the important conversation and, therefore, pressed his ear harder at the door.

The head of military operations, Mr Schmidt, said, "Any clues? We have to be cautious. You know? I heard from one of your officers that a group of boys have some information."

The Chief of Police, Mr Mertens, replied casually, "No real information. A few boys came to the police station and said that something was suspicious. I don't think they have any relevant information."

"Call them at once," Mr Schmidt said excitedly. "I don't think there is any sense in what they are saying," Mr Mertens again mentioned casually.

Hearing the whole conversation, Johann knocked at the door and entered the room. Both men were startled by his sudden entry. Johann said, "Excuse me, Mr Schmidt. I couldn't stop myself from overhearing, but I am one of the boys. We have important information that we want to tell you. I'm Johann. I'll call the other boys too and be back in about an hour to tell you the whole story." Mr Sebastian Schmidt nodded, "OK, sure, let's meet." Mr Ruediger Mertens did not seem excited to call the boys, but he kept quiet.

Sebastian Schmidt was a man of about five feet and ten inches in height, clean-shaven, and with a pleasant smile and kind eyes. Mr Schmidt was the head of the military establishment since it started operations in Nordreich. The operations had recently commenced in the new building, which had been constructed in place of an old, haunted mansion. This new building, with a modern exterior, also looked a bit out of place in the midst of the old town.

Johann rushed out of the compound and told Albert and Jurgen, "Let us all gather here in an hour," and then ran towards the police station to call his friends. Phillip was sitting on a bench outside the police station when Johann called, "Come with me." Meanwhile, Albert and Jurgen rushed to the beach and shouted at Manuel and Bastian, "Come fast."

They gathered outside the military establishment, and Johann told, "The head of this operation, Mr Sebastian Schmidt wants to

 The Mystery of the Military Establishment

Johann entered the room of the Head of
the Military Establishment, Mr Sebastian Schmidt,
while the Chief of Police, Mr Ruediger Mertens, looked on

question us about our suspicions." The boys were excited and happy. They wanted to rush in, but a guard came and stopped them and told sternly, "Hold on, kids. No one's allowed inside."

"We've got permission from the head of this operation, Mr. Sebastian Schmidt, to be inside. He wants to question us. We reported some suspicious activity, and he wants to know about it," Johann replied.

"Permission, you say?" The guard's eyes narrowed unbelievingly.

The guard called his fellow guard, "Hey, Mats. Tell the boss that a couple of kids have come and are claiming that he gave permission to meet them." Mats went up and asked Mr Schmidt, "Sir, some kids have come saying you gave them permission to come in. Shall we let them in?" Mr Schmidt replied, "Yes, I did give them permission to come and meet me."

Mats hurried down, and the outside guard shouted at him, "Well, what did he say?" "Calm down, Sean. The boss said he gave permission," Mats explained to the outside guard. "Sure, well, whatever the boss says," answered Sean. The outside guard, Sean, turned to the boys and apologised, "Sorry about that, but we have to be cautious, you know." The boys were let in, and Sean said to his fellow guard, "Mats, take them to the head's office."

Mats led the boys to the office and knocked. "Come in," Mr Schmidt replied. "Sir. The boys," Mats said. "Thank you, Mats. You may leave now," Mr Schmidt said.

Sebastian Schmidt turned to address the boys and said, "Well, for those of you who don't know me, I'm Sebastian Schmidt, and I'm in charge of this military establishment. You can now tell me your story." The boys had taken an immediate liking to Mr Schmidt. The boys relayed their story and the details of the three suspicious men.

Mr Schmidt said after patiently listening to the boys, "Very suspicious. Those men could be Carl Retz and his brother Paul Retz. Carl works as a guard, and Paul is an electrician in this establishment. They are from South America. The man that you saw on the yacht and in this establishment could be Gary Lenk. He works in the lab of our establishment."

"If you don't mind my asking. May I ask you, Sir? What is the secrecy about this military establishment?" Johann asked.

Sebastian Schmidt sighed and said, "I suppose you have a right to ask. After all, you brought this information, which is very useful. Okay, I'll tell you. You know NATO? The famous North Atlantic Treaty Organisation. NATO is working on a very secret military project which could help all democratic countries of the world, and it chose Germany to execute it. The government in Berlin chose Nordreich, as it is a remote village in northern Germany. Somehow, the news must have leaked out to foreign countries, and they would have hired spies to steal the secrets. I am here to oversee the design of a range of specialised military equipment based on a newly developed technology. The equipment would be manufactured at an undisclosed location and can be used to maintain peace in friendly countries. However, this equipment can be very harmful if misused. I'm also here to prevent any secrets from going out. I am afraid I cannot tell you more." Mr Schmidt then said, "Okay, that's the detail for you. Keep this information with you only. If you all have more information, do let me know."

The boys thanked the head of operations and promised to keep telling him of any new developments. The boys left the establishment thinking what should their next step be.

After all, they were the *Adventurers*. They needed to do something to save the secrets of this military establishment before it could fall into the wrong hands.

Chapter 4

Police on Whose Side?

The boys awoke early the next day and decided to go out to the town to enjoy the day.

While the boys were walking in the old town, they bumped into the Chief of Police, Mr Mertens, who was not very happy seeing the boys. He said unexcitedly, "Oh, it's you kids. I was about to send a message to you. Mr Schmidt wants to meet you."

"Why is the head of the establishment, Mr. Schmidt, calling us again?" Johann asked. "How do I know?" Mr Mertens replied again unexcitedly and added, "Now come quickly." The boys were puzzled and thought about it on the way walking towards Mr Schmidt's office.

"This Police Chief, Mr Mertens, sure is grumpy. He doesn't like it that we are called by Mr Schmidt," Manuel whispered to Albert, who nodded.

The boys were surprised as they were led out of the town through the southern side, where there was a forest. They went inside the forest and were then led to a small hut.

Police Chief Ruediger Mertens opened the door of the hut, and inside it, the boys saw a man with his back to the door. The head of the establishment, Mr Schmidt, turned suddenly and said, "Who are you? Oh, it's you guys. I wanted to have a word with you."

Mr Mertens turned to leave. Mr Schmidt said, "No Ruediger, stay. You are the Chief of Police." Mr Schmidt said to the boys, "I thought once again yesterday night about our meeting. I agree with you. We will follow the three suspicious men as you say."

"Really," Johann started speaking excitedly, but Ruediger interrupted, "What, Sebastian? I thought we agreed their story was nonsense. They pretend to be adventurers solving mysteries, as in a movie. You believe them?

They are kids. It's a fairy tale they want us to believe in."

Mr Schmidt patiently explained, "Ruediger, calm down. I have told you. We have to follow every lead."

"Okay, now that's settled. We will follow these suspicious guys," Mr Schmidt said. "Also, sorry about how Mr Mertens brought you to the forest, but we have to be cautious. I called you boys because I wanted to follow the clues you told me."

Police Chief Mr Mertens said, "Fine, I'll put our policemen to follow the three suspicious men, Paul Retz, Carl Retz and Gary Lenk. I'll also put policemen to quietly watch the yacht." Mr Schmidt said, "Ruediger, thanks for your time. You can now go back to your office for your meetings."

Mr Schmidt addressed the boys after Mr Mertens had left, "Come back tomorrow with a plan. I hear you call yourselves the *Adventurers*. And yes. One more point. I'd like you to meet my son Andreas." "Andreas," Mr Schmidt called excitedly. "Coming, father," replied Andreas from inside. They saw a boy who was around fifteen years old and had black hair. He looked quite similar to his father. The same smile and gentleness.

Mr Schmidt continued, "I'm leaving for Berlin right now, and I want you to spend time with my son Andreas. He is just like you boys. You also take care of him. His mother is not here at the moment." Saying this, Sebastian Schmidt left the hut for Berlin. "Okay, Bye," replied Andreas while waving to his father.

Johann and the other boys talked a lot with Andreas. Then Johann suddenly asked, "Where is your mother?" "She's on a yacht with some other people to make a business deal," Andreas replied. "What's the name of that yacht," Johann asked. "*The Barnet Sleuth*. Why do you ask?" Andreas replied. Johann happily said, "That's the same yacht on which our parents are also on. I think I met your mother once, Andreas." Andreas and the six boys kept talking and enjoyed their time together.

Suddenly, Police Chief Ruediger Mertens was seen rushing back into the hut and said, "You seven, come with us. Something urgent has happened." The boys went with him, and he took them to the hospital in the centre of the town.

Mr Mertens said, "The yacht with your parents on board collided with another yacht, which strayed off course. Unfortunately, people on board including your parents got hurt. The parents who got hurt include Mr Hanise, Mr and Mrs Manste and Mrs Schmidt. They're in the hospital now."

The boys nervously went inside the hospital and saw their parents there. While the others expressed sympathy over the injured people, Johann led his father away to a side. "Dad, did you see the name of the yacht which collided with your yacht?" Johann asked. "The name? Well, it was *The Southern Star*. Why?" replied Johann's father. *The Southern Star* made Johann dumbfounded. It was the same yacht the boys had been following. "What are you up to?" Johann's father asked. "Oh, just curious," was Johann's casual reply.

"Did you see who all were there on the yacht?" Johann further asked his father. "There were four men on the yacht. They quickly took their yacht away after they hit our yacht," Johann's dad replied.

The presence of fourth man on the yacht was new information for Johann.

The boys came out of the hospital after meeting their parents. They were sad that their parents had got hurt but were relieved that they were safe.

Suddenly, Johann said, "Look over there." "Yeah, what's going on?" Jurgen added. There was a crowd around the bank next to the hospital. They asked one nearby policeman, "What's going on?" He replied, "Mr. Sebastian Schmidt's safe is broken into. You know he is head of the military establishment." "He's my dad, I'm Andreas Schmidt," Andreas exclaimed.

"What was in your dad's locker, Andreas?" Johann asked softly. "This is dad's official locker. Given by his office when the construction commenced in the new building. I think it would have some important documents. Maybe some military secrets," replied Andreas in a soft tone.

Johann said to Andreas, "Just wondering if this is also done by those suspicious men?" Andreas replied, "Very strange. The locker has been there for some time, and this has happened now."

Andreas asked the policeman, "Any other locker also broken into?" The policeman replied, "No, only Mr. Schmidt's." "How did the thieves look like," Johann asked the policeman. The policeman described the face of one man. It seemed like one of the men seen by Johann on *The Southern Star* yacht.

"Let's go back to the hut in the woods and check if all is fine," Andreas suggested. The seven boys went and found that the hut was also broken into. "I'll call the Police Chief, Mr Mertens," Andreas said. "No, don't do it," Johann exclaimed. "Why?" Andreas asked, surprised by Johann's statement. "We do not completely trust the Police Chief. Who else knew about your dad's location?" Johann said. "Not many," replied Andreas. Phillip interrupted, "So you mean Police Chief Mr Mertens could be a spy?" Johann answered, "Maybe somebody could have followed your father, or maybe Mr Mertens is a spy. Let's check if the thief left any clues."

The boys searched the hut. Suddenly, Jurgen shouted, "Look over here." Johann rushed and reached first and said to the others, "It's a glove. The thief must have dropped it. He would have worn it to avoid detection of any fingerprints. Let's hide and see if he comes back to take the glove. The inside of the glove will have his fingerprints. The thief may come back. Andreas, Phillip, and Bastian, stay outside and tell us if anyone's coming." The three boys went out and hid behind the hut on the far side. The others stayed inside and hid in some quiet corners. Jurgen near the front door, Albert on the right side of the hut near a window in a small room, Manuel hid underneath a bed, and Johann at the back door behind a sofa. They blocked all four ways of escape for anyone who would come into the hut. It was a trap for the thief.

Johann said to the others, "Let's see what he came for and then only attack him. Keep something like a weapon with you. He may be armed." The boys each kept a chair or some rod near them and were ready to attack them. After some time, someone very quietly entered and picked up the glove and some papers. Then he was looking through the back door, thinking which way to go out.

Johann pounced on the thief and pushed him to the floor, and the others tied him up.

"Now tell us why you are here?" said Jurgen. As he turned the thief over, Jurgen exclaimed, "Karl Harse."

Karl Harse was an eighteen-year-old boy from the same school as most of the boys. Karl was a bully but a simpleton. He could be very easily manipulated. He was Johann's enemy at school. Johann was popular and clever, while Karl was neither. Karl saw them and burst out spluttering, "You thief, what are you doing here." Johann replied calmly, even though he was puzzled, "We are not thieves. You are the thief, and you explain to us."

Karl said, "I am also not a thief, my friends. I'll tell you the whole story. I regularly go to the docks, and the Captain of *The Southern Star* yacht has hired me for small jobs. He told me to go to this hut and take all the papers. He said it was his house." Johann said, "Be more careful, you were being manipulated. The owner of this hut will make your life very difficult for you if you come here again. Go now before I call him."

Chapter 5

The Police Chief, Mr Mertens' Loyalty?

The boys went home, thinking about the incident with the intruder in the hut, Karl Harse. On the way home, Johann told the others, "Don't tell the Police Chief, Mr Mertens, about the things we learnt. I don't trust him." He later added, "The gang on *The Southern Star* yacht sure is up to something bad."

The boys went home and decided to go to bed; Johann was so tired he was the first to fall into bed. He thought, "Nothing can wake me up tonight." So did all the other boys. But Johann was wrong. Something would wake him up that night. The clock chimed three o'clock, and Johann seemed to have heard the soft sound of the opening of a door.

It was a big house of Johann's parents, who had allowed Johann and his friends to stay when they were away. Andreas had also come with the boys to stay the night. It was a double-storey house. Andreas, Bastian, and Phillip were sleeping soundly on the ground floor, unaware of any sound. Johann peered through the staircase and distinctly caught the shape of a big, bulky figure of a man. Johann sneaked down the staircase and punched the man, knocking him out with an uppercut. Johann called the others, and they saw that the man who entered the house was none other than the Police Chief, Mr Mertens.

"What are you doing here?" said a shocked Johann. Mr Mertens seemed embarrassed but quickly gathered back his attitude and said, "I was called in this neighbourhood by my team on duty. I heard some noises from this house. So, I came to check if people of this house are all right. Maybe I was misinformed," and with that, he quickly left. "He's lying. He's a spy. You were right, Johann. He had come here to scare us or look for something in your house," Jurgen said angrily. A general murmur of agreement sounded in the group.

The boys went back to sleep and woke up late. They had a quiet breakfast, still shaken by the events of the previous night. They discussed about what they should do next. Johann said, "Let's go to the police station and do some spying on the Police Chief, Mr Mertens, and get some more information about the yacht and the men. I have a feeling he's hiding something from us."

"Yeah, let's go," Albert agreed. The boys quietly went to the police station and saw a guard posted outside. His name was Lothar Zepl. He was a nineteen-year-old burly lad. He used to be in school with them but had completed his studies and left school. Lothar and some of the boys used to be good friends, having played together in the same school team. Johann greeted him, "Hey." Lothar snapped out of his daze and said, "Oh hey! It's you guys. How's school, and who's this new guy," said Lothar excitedly while pointing to Andreas.

Johann introduced, "Lothar, this is Andreas. Andreas, this is Lothar. Now Lothar," turning to address him, Johann said, "Never mind about our school. It's all fine but what about you? Shouldn't you be in college. Why, at the police station?" It was a well-known fact that Lothar wanted to go to college. Lothar shrugged and said, "I am now working. I couldn't afford to pay for college. I'm on the job as a guard in this police station." Lothar asked, "Why are you here? Can I help you in some way?"

"We need one special help for old time's sake. It's something serious about the military establishment," Johann said and further added, "We're also working on a spy job. If you don't tell Mr Mertens, we will tell you all about it. We don't trust him, and I promise we'll tell you all we know." Lothar listened carefully but hesitated to say something. Johann thought, "Poor guy doesn't want to betray his boss. He'll be in so much trouble if Police Chief Mr Mertens found out." Lothar eventually said, "I also do not trust Mr Mertens. I promise not to tell him if you are doing something good." With all the guys staring at him in disbelief, he said, "I'm not lying. I promise I won't tell." Johann agreed, "You know what? I think we can trust him." Johann relayed the story of the suspicious people and the military establishment to Lothar, who immediately said, "I'll help you." Johann agreed with the idea of Lothar helping them, as they might need him and did not have any other option and said, "Thanks, buddy."

Lothar suddenly asked, "But why did you come to the police station?"

Jurgen replied, "To ask if Mr Mertens and the policemen have got any leads." Lothar said wistfully, "Seems like you do have clues to follow. As far as I am aware, the police team doesn't have any leads. I am not sure what Police Chief Mr Mertens knows." Johann asked curiously, "Why? What's Mr Mertens put you on?" Lothar replied, "All of us are on some other duty. So, we get to know nothing of this case." Johann asked, "What about Police Chief Mr Mertens?" Lothar said, "No, he does not do anything. He just sits in his office and does nothing for this case. But he goes out to the sea on a yacht. I think it's the same yacht that was mentioned by you – *The Southern Star*." "*The Southern Star*," exclaimed Jurgen and said, "That's the yacht which has been involved in all these suspicious activities. This puts a serious doubt in Mr Mertens's truthfulness. He's not listening to our clues. He must be a part of the gang."

Andreas got angry at the thought that Mr Mertens was double-crossing many people, including his father. According to Andreas, Mr Mertens was a deceitful fellow and part of the gang and thus didn't deserve to be the Chief of Police. Johann sensed Andreas' feelings and signalled Andreas to be quiet.

Johann was struck by a horrible idea that Mr Mertens, who was the Chief of Police, was allowed inside the military establishment. He could easily steal secrets, and nobody would even suspect him. He shared his thoughts with others. Jurgen agreed and said, "That's why he would have come to our house to search for any information we might have found."

Andreas was really angry by now and said, looking towards the Police Chief's office, "Mr Mertens, where are you? Come out and face me. I am Andreas Schmidt, son of Sebastian Schmidt, head of the military establishment." Johann whispered, "Andreas, don't let him know we're on his tail." As they went to Mr Mertens's office, policemen necks craned in their direction. Fortunately, Andreas' anger had calmed down. They reached the office of Mr Mertens and went in.

Johann said, "Hello, Chief. Any luck with the clues we told you?" Mr Mertens turned away from them, embarrassed and said, "To be honest, kids, I have a lot on my mind about the military establishment, and your clues were nothing. You are all wasting my time."

"What?" Johann retorted, pretending to be angry. It was all part of the plan they had discussed. Johann had said earlier while the boys were making the plan, "He'll say no. Then we'll pretend to be upset and force him to do something. If my hunch is correct and if he is part of the gang, he'll not do anything against the gang. In that case, we'll stop telling him any further clues. If he's innocent, he will start acting against the gang. In that case, we'll keep telling him the clues." Johann continued, "Mr Mertens, you please arrest these people." "Yes, Sir. We all feel you should investigate further in this case," Andreas further added. Mr Mertens, who was visibly irritated by the last few statements, said, "Hey, kids, don't go to such an extent to push me. Let me think again," and he went out of his room. The boys exchanged glances. They waited, and after two minutes, Mr Mertens came and said,

"I again thought about your story, but it is not convincing. You go away, or else I will arrest you boys."

The boys quietly walked back home from the police station. Johann said, "Now we *Adventurers* will do it ourselves along with the military establishment head, Mr Schmidt, and with no outside interference from police. Actually, I'm glad we got rid of a deceitful thief like Police Chief Mertens."

Johann thought for some time and said, "You know what I'm going to do? Call Robert and Thomas Kinch, our school friends. Their father works at a premium security agency, and he may have some information. More so, these brothers are good at computers and various electronic gadgets." Johann told Bastian to go to the Kinch brothers' home and give his message, as they stayed close to Bastian's home.

Robert was fifteen years old, and Thomas was nineteen years old. Bastian told them, "Hey Robert and Thomas, we need some information about the military establishment. It's an important case. Please meet us tomorrow at Johann's home around eleven o'clock in the morning. Johann specially requested for you both." "Sure," agreed the brothers.

Robert and Thomas were initially worried that something wrong had happened. Then, they thought it might just be a prank, but they decided to go as they trusted both Johann and Bastian. Robert was very good at computers and radio transmission, while Thomas was good at mechanical machines. On the way, Robert asked his brother, "Thomas, do you think this case that Johann mentioned is connected to our father's case at the military establishment?" Thomas replied, "I'm not sure." When they reached Johann's house, both Robert and Thomas were shocked to see the boys looking worried. Johann shouted in excitement, "Wow, it's Robert and Thomas." Robert asked, "Which case did you call us for?" Johann told them the whole story about the military establishment. Robert and Thomas replied, "We'll help you," and they joined the boys in making plans to catch the thieves.

Chapter 6

Middle of the Night Adventure

The boys were continuing to stay at the home of Johann's parents. His parents had left for another business trip after recovering. It had become the temporary home for the six *Adventurers* along with Andreas and also the place for them to plan their actions.

"Wake up, Jurgen," Andreas said, throwing a pillow at him. Jurgen woke up in a flash, shouting, "What happened."

"Nothing happened. It is already nine-thirty in the morning," Andreas said. "Come and have breakfast," Andreas said smilingly. Jurgen dressed and went down, and he saw all of them sitting around the table having breakfast. Jurgen, having woken up from his sleep, scanned the table and saw only six people, including himself, on the table.

"Someone's missing? It's Johann. He must be sleeping. I'll wake him up. I'm just going to go up the staircase and call him down," Jurgen said. "Okay, go up," said Andreas. Jurgen knocked on the door once. No answer. Twice, no answer. Third time, no answer. Finally, being unable to stand it, he pushed the door open and saw no one was there. In fact, it seemed that nobody had slept on Johann's bed. Jurgen rushed down the stairs and fell. Bastian laughed. Jurgen looked like he wanted to hit Bastian. Albert saw this and intervened by asking, "What happened?" Jurgen said, "Johann's not there. It seems that his bed was not slept in."

Johann had gone out in the middle of the night when it was raining. He had remembered the words of the man in charge of the yachts who had told them that the yacht, *The Southern Star*, came late at midnight. So, he decided to get some information about the yacht. He wore a coat and typical fisherman's clothes. Johann also took a mini camera and slipped it in his coat. He went on the shore and found *The Southern Star* had docked. Johann went close to some people standing near the yacht and heard, "Need to complete this job tonight. We'll call this fellow."

"Hey, You. What's your name," shouted Gary, the person standing next to the yacht, to Johann. Johann replied, "Just call me John," disguising his name to hide suspicions. Gary said, "You, John, can you help on the boat? You will have to help with small jobs, and we will pay you good money." "Yes," Johann said, jumping at the chance and hardly believing his good luck. "What do I need to do? Where are we going? How many people are on the yacht, and which yacht are we going on?" Johann continued. Gary said sternly, "You need to be a helper. You can do it, right? No questions." Johann answered, "Oh yeah, I can do it." Gary answered, "Okay, then just go on the boat. The one there is called *The Southern Star*."

Johann excitedly climbed on the yacht and saw a few other men on the yacht. "Hey Carlo," Gary said, addressing the Captain. "Yeah," Carlo said. "I got you a helper for small jobs," Gary said. Johann smartly carried out all jobs assigned to him on the yacht. They soon reached another coast after sailing for some time. Gary told Johann his job was done and also gave him some money.

The people got off the yacht, and Johann also saw a person who shocked him. It was none other than the Police Chief, Mr Mertens. Johann could not believe it. He became completely convinced that the Police Chief was working with the gang.

Johann became very angry but soon regained his composure. He looked around the yacht and realised that he was alone at that time. He sneaked around on the yacht and found a diary. He could not believe his good luck, and he took it and quietly went out of the yacht. He wandered for some distance away from the yacht until he met a man and asked him, "Which town am I in?" The man looked puzzled at such a question and replied, "Why? it's Bremerhaven." Johann said, "Thanks," and rushed off. He thought and drew up a mental map and said to himself, "Okay, I'm in Bremerhaven, which is about 35 km from home." He started walking. Johann walked for quite some time till he was able to get a ride back on a pick-up truck going that side. Then again, he had to walk some more distance to reach home.

Meanwhile, Johann's friends were worried about Johann. Albert had organised the team to look for their friend, Johann. Bastian and Phillip were checking for clues in Johann's room. Andreas was searching on the beach, while Jurgen and Manuel tried searching in the town. All the boys came back to Johann's home with no concrete information.

Albert was thinking about where else to search and was on the porch of the house, worried about Johann. Suddenly, he saw Johann coming and called out to others. Johann somehow reached the steps of the house and almost fainted from fatigue. Albert was shocked by what he saw. Johann looked really tired and sick. Albert helped him inside and assisted him to a couch to rest.

Soon, Johann got up and drank some water and juice. Feeling better, he told the others his story. The boys were amazed by the information and specially of the presence of Police Chief, Mr Mertens, at *The Southern Star* yacht. Johann asked, "Andreas, do you know when your father will come back to Nordreich? Is there any way to contact him?" "No," was the reply from Andreas.

Chapter 7

The Final Plan

The *Adventurers*, along with Andreas, woke up early the next day at Johann's house and met up with the other three boys – Thomas, Robert, and Lothar – for breakfast at their favourite café. They pondered about what to do next, after the previous day's events. Johann thought for a long time and said, "Let's go to the secret hut of Mr. Schmidt, the head of the military establishment. I have a feeling some military documents may be in danger with the gang planning something fishy along with the Police Chief, Mr Mertens. Also, we might find some new clues as well." The boys walked fast and in silence and soon reached the hut.

To their shock, the boys found the door was open. "Oh no. I hope the thieves didn't come again," Johann said and rushed towards the door. "Guys, come," he shouted with a poker face. The others did not know whether Johann was shouting from fear or joy or maybe a bit of both. They rushed in and saw Mr Schmidt sitting with his back to them. "Chief," Johann shouted. Mr Schmidt turned and smiled and said, "How's it going?" Johann replied, "Things are not going so well. The gang is becoming more bolder, and so are we. I have a feeling they are planning something huge. We also doubt the integrity of Police Chief Mr Mertens." He relayed the story so far. Johann paced up and down and said, "I have an idea. It may work, but it's risky. It could make the thieves fall for it, but I'm not sure." Mr Schmidt smiled and said, "Worth a serious thought for sure."

Johann asked in a serious tone, "We now need to catch the people who are behind all this. Chief, what do you think this gang is after?" Military establishment Chief, Mr Schmidt, explained, "Any gang will want the details of this new military equipment. I mean, it's the blueprint and other information so that they can replicate it. The blueprint has all specifications and key drawings."

Johann excitedly laid out his idea, "We need to catch the gang with some document or blueprint as bait. We put out a blueprint of one important military equipment, which is a really important document. But it's fake, so let them steal it. And then we'll catch them." Andreas added, "Good thought. We will have to plan this without the Police Chief, Mr Mertens. We do not trust him."

Mr Schmidt thought for a long time and then agreed. "Okay, sounds like a good plan. We will be able to catch the gang if the plan works. I need to also arrange for a fake blueprint. We also need to involve our military police instead of Mr. Mertens and his police force. We only have a few military policemen, so you boys have to work with them. I will tell my head office in Berlin of this plan, too."

Johann then continued with his friends, "We'll each have some roles to play. Albert and Andreas will have to work with the military policemen to go to the yacht. Jurgen will track them on the way, and Manuel will notify us when the gang starts to go. Lothar will notify us when *The Southern Star* yacht docks. The distance between the hut and the docks is about two kilometres. There will be main points where some of you will stay. Phillip at the supermarket. Thomas at the mall. Bastian at the police station, and Robert at the sports complex. I will stay next to *The Southern Star* yacht and alert the military policemen by whistling. Then they'll arrest the men. All of us will use walkie-talkies to alert each other." "Excellent," Mr Schmidt said. "I will speak to my head office in Berlin. I'll arrange the fake blueprint and walkie-talkies, and I'll tell my military policemen the plan," he said.

The next day, the head of the military establishment, Mr Schmidt, confirmed to the boys that he had spoken to his head office in Berlin. He also arranged a team of military police. Mr Schmidt called the boys and the military police to his secret hut for the final plan. He told the boys, "You go ahead with the plan. Nobody other than us should know anything. I have explained everything to the military police team. They will support you as per plan. And here's the fake copy of the blueprint that the gang is after. Also, here are your walkie-talkies." Mr Schmidt got serious and said, "Remember, we need to catch them doing something wrong." Johann jumped and said, "Sure, Chief, we want them to steal the fake document, and we will catch them. Then you ask them what all the gang is up to." Mr Schmidt smiled while saying, "Agreed. Let's do it. You boys get on with your work. All the best."

All the boys were ready and excited to have the military police instead of Police Chief Mr Mertens. The boys finalised the remaining points of the plan. The fake blueprint was kept in the hut. Mr Schmidt suddenly said, "How will we inform the gang of *The Southern Star* of this fake blueprint." Johann immediately replied, "We will leak it to Police Chief, Mr Mertens. This will also show us his integrity. If the gang comes to the hut, we will catch them."

Andreas, Mr Schmidt's son, excitedly explained, "I will go and tell the Police Chief Mr Mertens that my dad had to go to Berlin head office. I think he has left a blueprint in the hut." Johann jumped with joy and said, "This is a good plan. Andreas, you go and somehow bump into Police Chief Mr Mertens and tell him about the blueprint."

Johann said to others, "Let's hide outside next to the hut and also inside the hut, and follow anyone who comes to steal the blueprint."

In a few hours, Andreas called on the walkie-talkie, "Hey, I somehow told the Police Chief, Mr Mertens, that there is a blueprint in the hut." "How was his reaction?" Johann asked. Andreas replied, "He looked happy after he heard this."

The boys waited anxiously for the remaining part of the day and the night. Some boys slept inside the hut, and military police quietly hid outside the hut. The other boys were at their positions at various places to track the gang once they stole the fake blueprint.

The next day morning, the boys got up sleepily. Johann asked, "Oh, it seems nobody came yesterday to steal the fake blueprint." Andreas added, "Does it mean Police Chief Mr Mertens is not passing information?" Johann replied, "Mr Mertens is surely involved. Let's wait one more day." The boys quietly remained in the hut the whole day while eating food available inside the hut. The other boys waited at their locations. The night fell, and still nobody came. Johann said sadly, "Have we lost this case? Nobody is coming?" The boys could not sleep in the night and grew more worried. Andreas said, "Oh, it's about to be morning soon. Still, nobody has come."

Suddenly, Johann said, "All quiet. I hear something." The hut door opened, and two men quietly sneaked in. They used torch lights to look around while opening drawers and stopped in front of the drawer that mentioned *'Important Documents'*. One person whispered, "Open the drawer. It may be inside this." The other person opened the drawer and excitedly said, "Got it." The men started to make their way out. Andreas almost got up to catch the thieves, and Johann held his arm and whispered, "Let them go."

After the men left the hut with the fake blueprint, Johann said, "We need to follow them. Let's action our plan now. Please start tracking them on the walkie-talkies."

All the boys sprang into action to carry out their part of the plan. Albert said to the military policemen, who were wearing plain clothes and were acting like normal people, "Please,

Sir, come over here and be ready." Meanwhile, Jurgen shouted out, "Manuel, where are you?"

Manuel used the walkie-talkie and said, "Phillip, the two thieves are coming your way towards the edge of the forest." Phillip waited, and after ten minutes, the two thieves reached the edge of the forest. Phillip said, "Thomas, they are now coming your way." Thomas soon saw them and alerted Bastian. When the men came where Bastian was waiting, he alerted Robert. When the men went past Robert, he said, "Johann, they are now reaching the beach," and Lothar said, "Johann, *The Southern Star* yacht has docked."

Johann quickly came from another route from the hut towards the beach in a fast car belonging to military police. Johann was on high alert, and he quickly spotted the thieves and said, "There they are." Andreas shouted, "Albert, here." As the two thieves parked their car close to *The Southern Star* yacht, the boys led the plainclothes military policemen, who were hiding behind some rocks, to the thieves. The military policemen caught the thieves before they could reach the yacht and said to them, "You're under arrest."

The boys asked the two thieves for information, but the thieves stubbornly refused. Johann said, "We know about Carlo, okay." "Yeah, and M…," Andreas started speaking, but was stopped because of a sharp jab in the ribs by Johann. The boys left the thieves with the military police. Thereafter, Andreas asked Johann, "Why did you stop me from talking about Police Chief Mr Mertens' name?" Johann said, "Mr Mertens will come to interrogate them, and these two men will tell him that we're on his tail."

Johann said, "These two men are saying nothing, but we now need to catch the whole gang and understand the motive." Andreas added, "It is clear *The Southern Star* is the key to solving this case."

Meanwhile, the military establishment Chief, Mr Schmidt, also reached the beach and went to the boys. Johann told Mr Schmidt, "Chief, *The Southern Star* yacht is being used by the gang. We have proof now. The two thieves who stole the fake blueprint were going to *The Southern Star* yacht. We need to now catch the whole gang."

Mr Schmidt explained to the boys, "Carefully go on the yacht, with military police in plain clothes supporting you from outside. Let's see what the gang on the yacht wants. We have to also catch them red-handed." "Yes, Chief," replied Johann, "we will do without anybody knowing."

Mr Schmidt told the military policemen not to take the two thieves to the police station, but to his hut for interrogation.

Chapter 8

The Dangerous Gang

The boys' next job was to get hold of the dangerous gang. In the meantime, all the boys had reached the beach. Johann said, "The secrets are on *The Southern Star* yacht. This is proved now. We now need to find out the secrets." Andreas said, "We need to quickly check this yacht and see what is there." Johann added, "We also need to catch Police Chief Mr Mertens."

Johann said, "Let's now get on *The Southern Star* yacht. Let's try and get some job on the yacht. There are only a few members of the gang on the yacht. Hence, they will need helpers. Also, we have caught two of their men." Johann pointed out, "When I was taken as a helper, they took some others also. Let's present ourselves as a team of helpers capable of doing many jobs. In this way, nobody will doubt us."

Johann further explained to his friends, "Lothar, Robert, Manuel, Bastian, Phillip, Thomas, Jurgen, Albert, Andreas – We all should try and work as helpers in whichever area they need people. Each one of us can work as a mechanic, technician, lookout man, radioman or chef. They may need three, four or more of us. However, as many as they want can go on the yacht, and the remaining can just stay on the beach and keep an eye from outside." Johann further added, "And Robert, you try to be the radioman. Tell Mr Schmidt about any new developments from the yacht. Robert, you have the most important job – to tell our whereabouts to Mr Schmidt."

The boys went along with Johann to Gary, who was identifying people as helpers. Johann said, "Hello, I hope you remember me. I had worked on the yacht as a helper. We again heard that you needed some more helpers." "Yes, we do need helpers. We need people to help in many sections and do various jobs. We need helpers such as mechanic, technician, lookout man, radio man, chef and also for help in navigating the yacht," answered Gary. The boys happily replied, "Chief, we can help with all these jobs." The boys quickly boarded *The Southern Star* yacht. Soon, Gary started giving them various jobs, and the boys smartly started executing them.

As per the plan, while some of the boys were talking to Gary, the others sneaked inside into different parts of the yacht. They went into an isolated room underneath and saw a heavy crate. Robert asked, "What do you suppose are the crates for?" "Maybe parts to build the weapon and firepower. It has some signs on the crate that indicate that," Johann answered. "Firepower?" Andreas asked in amazement. The boys went on doing their jobs on the yacht, and each was looking out for something suspicious.

Robert was told by the ship's Captain, Carlo, "Hey you. You said you can be a radioman. Our radioman is sick today. Send a message. Send it to the police station at this frequency, and the message should mention – Meet us on the yacht at Bremerhaven harbour at three in the afternoon." Robert sent the message and then thought, "Oh. The message is going to Police Chief Mr Mertens. He is surely involved."

Meanwhile, Lothar was helping in cooking food and was told to serve the men. He went outside and listened at the door. The Captain of the yacht, Carlo, said to his partner, "Gary, I think those boys are spies, watch out for them."

Bastian and Phillip were told by the Captain of the yacht, Carlo, "Go back to your quarters." Thomas and Manuel were also told by Gary, "Back to your quarters." Jurgen was sneaking out, and he accidently tripped on one of the smaller crates. He looked inside the crate and saw some blueprints and a diary. He decided to check it later with the others. In the meantime, Manuel and Albert found the firepower of Chinese make inside some other crates. "Strange," Andreas thought, as he was seeing through another small crate and found some pictures and a contract agreement.

Johann was spying on the Captain of the yacht, Carlo, and his partner, Gary. Carlo said, "We'll go to Bremerhaven and tell Police Chief Mr Mertens about it. With him, we'll give the head of military establishment, Mr Mertens, a slip and steal it soon."

The boys went into the storage room in the corner of the yacht and conveyed to each other all the suspicious activities. Johann said in a hushed tone, "Makes me think they are planning something big soon." Lothar interrupted, "I think they suspect we are spies." For a moment, there was silence, and Johann said, "We have no choice now. Let's complete this. We better hide when Police Chief Mr Mertens comes on this yacht, and you guys disguise yourself. Now show me the pictures and the contract."

The picture showed five men shaking hands. They seemed like Chinese. The contract was signed by Chinese people with something written in Chinese under the signatures. The diary, which Johann had found last time on the yacht, also signalled a deal with Chinese people. Johann said, "They must have made a deal with China to steal something from the military establishment. That explains the Chinese firepower. Send it to Mr. Schmidt what we learnt, Robert." Robert sent the message to Mr Schmidt from the yacht itself.

At three p.m., the yacht docked at Bremerhaven and picked up Police Chief, Mr Mertens. He said to the Captain of the yacht,

Carlo, "We'll go for the meeting downstairs." Jurgen, on hearing this, whispered from inside the room, "Let's go and spy on these men." Jurgen, Albert and Andreas quietly stood outside the door, trying to listen. The Police Chief, Mr Mertens suddenly opened the door and found the three boys and brought them inside. "Stowaways, we'll dump you in the sea," Carlo said. Mr Mertens said, "One of them is Mr Schmidt's son. Chief of military establishment's son." Carlo said, "We'll keep him as a hostage and for ransom, and we'll dump the others as soon as we get into the sea and out of sight."

Johann was hearing this and thought that he had to somehow save his friends. The men tied the boys and then went up on the dock. At the first opportunity, Johann went inside the room, cut out the ropes with his pocket knife and told his friends, "Jump off the yacht and swim. We are quite close to the shore." The boys ran in the dark towards the end of the yacht, but the men felt their presence. They punched Johann, who stumbled, while the other boys jumped off into the water and started swimming. Johann hit a blow to the Captain of the yacht, Carlo, who fell down into the water. His partner, Gary, gave Johann a big blow, and Johann fell off to one side. Johann punched Gary, throwing him into the water.

The Police Chief, Mr Mertens, came at Johann with a knife and tried to scratch Johann's face. Johann crouched down and sprung up with such force, thereby making the knife fly out of Mr Merten's hand, and then punched his face. Mr Mertens stumbled, and Johann again punched Mr Mertens in the face, who fell down. Finally, Johann jumped into the water, and he swam away.

All the boys swam safely to the beach. Meanwhile, the head of the military establishment, Mr Schmidt, also reached the beach. He had received one of the boys, Robert's radio message from the yacht. The boys quickly told the whole story. Mr Schmidt came towards the boys and said, "I think we have sufficient proof. We need to catch all on *The Southern Star* yacht, including Police Chief, Mr Mertens."

The boys suddenly heard fast boats with sirens. "What are those dad?" asked Andreas to his father, Mr Schmidt. The Chief of the military establishment replied, "Coast guards. They will catch all of them in five minutes."

The boys could see from a distance the Coast Guard boats surrounding *The Southern Star* yacht.

The boys seemed happy, gave high-fives, and screamed in happiness. Even Mr Schmidt joined in the fun.

Suddenly, Mr Schmidt said in a serious tone, "Boys, great job. You are the real *Adventurers*. Go home and rest. I have serious work to do with the gang."

Chapter 9

The Final Surprise

The boys went to their own homes, missing the fun at Johann's house. The boys got up the next day in the morning, happy with what they had achieved. They once again met at their favourite café in the town.

Johann said, "I guess we can rightly call ourselves the *Adventurers*."

Andreas was the last to join at the café. He said, "My father wants to meet all of you at his office. Come, let's go now."

The boys excitedly walked towards the office of the Chief of the military establishment. Mr Schmidt looked tired and said, "I wanted to tell all of you that we worked the whole night, and the gang has been caught. We also have all the information about their plans and what they were up to."

Johann asked Mr Schmidt, "Chief, what was the gang up to?"

Mr Schmidt explained, "They wanted to steal the secrets and pass them on to the Chinese to make money. We are safe now." Johann said, "Chief, please tell us the whole story." Mr Schmidt continued, "The gang wanted the blueprints to sell to the Chinese. The Chinese were driving the whole operation from China. You remember I had told you. These blueprints are for the latest technology and military equipment. This is a very sophisticated military equipment that is used for peaceful purposes. But this equipment can be misused if fallen into the wrong hands. These people had already gained access to the military establishment. We are safe now. The whole gang is caught."

Johann asked, "Chief, what about the Chinese?" Mr Schmidt explained, "They were managing from China through the South American gang. The Chinese cannot do much without the gang."

Johann interrupted, "What happened to Police Chief Mr Mertens?" Sebastian became very serious and said, "I cannot tell you much. He is in trouble. Already, action has been initiated on him. He is in military police custody now."

Sebastian smiled and said, "You all did very good work. You are the true *Adventurers*. The head office in Berlin wants to award you." His son Andreas interrupted, "Guess where? They want us all to get an award at the head office. In Berlin." Mr Schmidt added, "The military head office will give you a special award each. The special gallantry awards. This is being given for the first time to young boys like you. You deserve it."

Johann tried to speak but could not speak. He was in shock. Also, all the other boys were in shock. Suddenly, they were heroes. Soon, they were surrounded by many people who applauded the boys.

Johann could finally speak, "Let's pack our bags for Berlin."

The special award in Berlin was the REAL SURPRISE to the boys.

Afterwards, Johann said to his friends, "I guess we really are the *Adventurers*."